The Montgomery Bus Boycott

PERSPECTIVES ON

The Montgomery Bus Boycott

Milestone of the Civil Rights Movement

KATIE MARSICO

Cavendish Square

Published by Cavendish Square Publishing, LLC

Library of Congress Cataloging-in-Publication Data
Marsico, Katie, 1980–
The Montgomery bus boycott : milestone of the civil rights movement / Katie Marsico.
p. cm. — (Perspectives on)
Includes bibliographical references and index.
Summary: "Provides comprehensive information on the Montgomery bus boycott in 1955 and the differing perspectives accompanying it"—Provided by publisher.
ISBN 978-1-60870-447-7 (print) 978-1-60870-719-5 (ebook)
1. Montgomery Bus Boycott, Montgomery, Ala., 1955–1956—Juvenile literature. 2. African Americans—Civil rights—Alabama—Montgomery—History—20th century—Juvenile literature. 3. Civil rights movements—Alabama—Montgomery—History—20th century—Juvenile literature. 4. Montgomery (Ala.)—Race relations—History—20th century—Juvenile literature. I. Title.
F334.M79N4538 2012
323.1196'073076147—dc22
2010033906

Editor: Christine Florie
Publisher: Michelle Bisson
Art Director: Anahid Hamparian
Series Designer: Sonia Chathatzbanian

Expert Reader: Tenisha Armstrong, Associate Director of the Martin Luther King, Jr., Research and Education Institute, Stanford, California

Photo research by Marybeth Kavanagh

Cover photo by AP Photo/Horace Cort

The photographs in this book are used by permission and through the courtesy of: The Bridgeman Art Library International: Pools of Defiance, 2001 (oil on canvas), Bootman, Colin (Contemporary Artist)/Private Collection, 2-3; Corbis: Bettmann, 8, 18; Everett Collection: 11, 73; The Granger Collection, NYC: 15; Getty Images: Popperfoto, 19; Don Cravens/Time Life Pictures, 32L, 43, 46, 63, 75; Michael Ochs Archives, 32R; Grey Villet/Time Life Pictures, 33, 60; National Archives/ Newsmakers, 83; Justin Sullivan, 87; AP Photo: 30, 55, 85; Gene Herrick, 34, 39; Perry Aycock, 79

Printed in the United States of America
1 3 5 6 4 2

Contents

Introduction

Even after the conclusion of the Civil War in 1865, African Americans had to struggle to win the freedoms guaranteed to all citizens by the U.S. Constitution. At various times and places, their efforts were challenged by discriminatory statutes known as Jim Crow laws, by the Ku Klux Klan and other informal associations often called hate groups, and even by a Supreme Court ruling that legitimized the idea of "separate but equal" institutions for blacks. On December 5, 1955, African Americans in Montgomery, Alabama, started a 381-day protest against segregation that reshaped the way men and women across the nation perceived civil rights. On that date, they began the Montgomery Bus Boycott in an effort to change municipal laws that required segregated seating on public transportation.

As Rosa Parks, Martin Luther King Jr., and other activists were waging their fight against city and bus company officials, long held social and political ideas dear to countless white southerners were being challenged. While African American perspectives were rooted in the desire for progress and improvement, white vantage points were often shaped by the need to maintain a world regulated by clear racial boundaries. With each side unwilling to compromise on certain fundamental issues related to bus segregation laws, violence frequently erupted in Montgomery, and boycotters were forced to consider new tactics.

Protestors therefore redefined their goals and strategies and ultimately, in 1956, brought their call for fair treatment to the highest court in the land. When Supreme Court justices handed down a ruling that rendered the segregation of Montgomery's buses unconstitutional, the path was paved for the civil rights movement, an era of activism and change. Along the way, men and women of various backgrounds used everything from peaceful demonstrations to firebombs and national legislation to express their viewpoints on racial integration. More than half a century after the Montgomery Bus Boycott transpired, it still is remembered for marking the onset of the civil rights movement. The perspectives of key players in this protest are essential to helping modern generations understand the words, actions, and emotions that shaped the battle for equal rights that began on an Alabama bus in 1955.

WAPX
1600 ON YOUR DIAL

One

Tired of Giving In

For forty-two-year-old Rosa Parks, December 1, 1955, did not initially seem as though it would prove extraordinary. Parks, who was employed as a seamstress, had spent most of the day working at a department store called Montgomery Fair in downtown Montgomery, Alabama. At the end of her shift each day, she boarded a bus at Cleveland Avenue to take her home. Like countless other African Americans, Rosa Parks relied upon the Montgomery City Lines for public transportation.

As was true in that era for most public facilities, including lunch counters and rest rooms, in much of the South the local bus system was segregated. Blacks were permitted to use the same buses as whites, but they were expected to follow certain rules. For example, they were not allowed to sit in the first ten seats located in the front of the vehicle, because these seats were exclusively reserved for white passengers.

African Americans were supposed to ride in the ten seats that filled the back of the bus. In between the white and "colored" sections were sixteen additional seats. While anyone could sit in this area, drivers routinely instructed black

Rosa Parks, sitting in the front of a bus in Montgomery, after the Supreme Court outlawed segregation on the city bus system on December 21, 1956.

riders to give up these seats and stand if a white passenger boarded the bus when the first ten seats were already filled.

Being ordered to stand was not an uncommon experience for African Americans. Montgomery City Lines drivers—all of whom were white—were also frequently in the habit of insisting that blacks pay their fare at the front of the bus, exit the vehicle, and then reenter through a different door at the back. Sometimes this ritual resulted in black passengers being cheated out of a ride. It was not unusual for a driver to accept money for a fare and then pull away before the rider boarded the bus in the rear.

Parks was familiar with such treatment. In fact, the driver of the bus she boarded on that December day in 1955 was the same man she had clashed with twelve years earlier. In 1943 Montgomery City Lines employee J. F. Blake had refused Parks a ride when she objected to the routine of paying in the front of the vehicle and reentering at the back; she was left in the pouring rain. Since that incident, she had tried to avoid his bus whenever possible.

When she boarded Blake's bus in 1955, she sat at the front of the middle section. As more and more people crammed into the vehicle, it was not long before the ten seats designated for white passengers were completely filled. As a result, Blake told Parks and three other black riders in her row to give up their spots and stand. While the other three followed the driver's instructions, Parks politely but firmly refused.

Blake responded by threatening to have Parks arrested, but she remained in her seat. Blake immediately exited the bus and found police officers, who proceeded to handcuff her. Authorities then booked, fingerprinted, and jailed Parks, who was charged with violating city codes related to racial segregation and "refusing to obey [the] orders of [the] bus driver." It was unlikely that at the time of her arrest, the Montgomery police department, Blake, or even Parks herself realized the impact that these events would have on civil rights.

Rosa Parks was arrested and fingerprinted in December 1955 for refusing to move to the back of the bus.

Inspiring a Revolution

Years after her historic ride on the Montgomery City Lines in December 1955, Rosa Parks emphasized that she had never planned to spark the boycott that followed her arrest. She explained many times that she was thinking of day-to-day trivialities when Blake ordered her to give up her seat. When the driver became insistent, however, Parks resolved to stand up for her rights.

"When I got on the bus that evening I wasn't thinking about causing a revolution or anything of the kind," she stated during a subsequent interview. "I was thinking about my husband. . . . I was hoping he'd had a good day. I was thinking about my back aching and about the pretty sights and sounds of Christmas. I was thinking about how we were going to have a good time this Christmas, and everybody was going to be happy. But when that white driver stepped back toward us, when he waved his hand and ordered us up and out of our seats, I felt a determination cover my body like a quilt on a winter night. I felt all the meanness of every white driver I'd seen who'd been ugly to me and other black people through the years I'd known on the buses in Montgomery. I felt a light suddenly shine through the darkness."

As Parks later recalled,

> I had no idea when I refused to give up my seat on that Montgomery bus that my small action would help put an end to the segregation laws in the South. People always say that I didn't give up my seat because I was tired, but that wasn't true. I was not tired physically, or no more tired than I usually was at the end of a working day. I was not old, although some people have an image of me as being old then. I was forty-two. No, the only tired I was, was tired of giving in.

Within days of Parks's arrest, she had gained the support of well-known African American activists, as well as the majority of the approximately 40,000 blacks who rode the city's buses. Just as important, the action taken in response to her situation challenged the rigid segregation policies that existed throughout Montgomery. The boycott of the local bus system was organized by leaders of the city's black community. It began on December 5, 1955, and lasted for 381 days.

Many activists initially hoped that the peaceful resistance—encouraging African American residents to rely on other means of transportation—would force the Montgomery City Lines to improve their treatment of black passengers. Not all the men and women who planned the boycott initially intended to completely undo segregation. Some simply aimed to win additional—rather than equal—rights for African American riders.

At about the same time as the Montgomery Bus Boycott, Americans expressed their opinions on segregation in many ways. Here, students protest school integration in Baltimore, Maryland, in 1955.

By the time the boycott concluded, their goal had become to eliminate all segregation on buses. Along the way, Americans with varying perspectives on racial equality voiced their opinions and expressed their emotions. The heated battle they fought over a segregated society stretched from Alabama jail cells to the U.S. Supreme Court.

Whatever motivations lay behind the Montgomery Bus Boycott, it appeared that African Americans across the nation were tired of giving in. The action they took in

December 1955 marked the beginning of the civil rights movement, which was rooted in the idea that citizens of all races were entitled to the freedoms and privileges outlined in the U.S. Constitution.

No Strangers to Segregation

A little less than a century before the Montgomery Bus Boycott, Americans had fought a civil war (1861–1865) over various issues, one of which was slavery. For the most part, white southerners were in favor of being allowed to own black slaves, while many northerners—whose troops ultimately won the conflict—opposed this practice. When the war concluded, Congress passed three amendments to the U.S. Constitution that were intended to safeguard the rights of African Americans.

Known as the Reconstruction Amendments, the Thirteenth, Fourteenth, and Fifteenth amendments were enacted between 1865 and 1870. The amendments were so named because, from 1865 to 1877, the United States was in the midst of an era commonly referred to as Reconstruction. During this period, U.S. leaders attempted to reorganize and restructure the states of the defeated Confederacy. From their perspective, redefining the role of African Americans in postwar southern society was essential.

The Thirteenth Amendment formally abolished slavery, the Fourteenth discussed the scope of constitutional rights African Americans were entitled to as U.S. citizens, and the Fifteenth stated that race should not be a factor in determining a person's voting privileges. For blacks who lived in the South, the Reconstruction Amendments often proved to be little more than mere words.

Still recovering from the catastrophic social and economic effects of losing the war, many white southerners were not anxious to promote the rights of men and women whom they were accustomed to regarding as not their equals. Consequently, African Americans in the South continued to experience oppression and prejudice.

One of the most significant examples of the racial inequality that black southerners faced came in the form of Jim Crow laws. Starting about 1876, these statutes—which were enacted at both state and local levels—supported unequal treatment of blacks and whites. Jim Crow laws assigned African Americans separate public facilities and services. From hospitals and schools to lunch counters and drinking fountains, practically any public setting was subject to a legalized dividing line between the races. Signs designated separate areas and services for "coloreds" and "Negroes," and terms such as "darky" and "nigger"—which are considered racist and insulting in modern times—were commonly used by whites in day-to-day conversation.

Jim Crow laws existed in other parts of the United States besides the South, though they were often stricter and more widely accepted in southern states that had been on the losing side of the Civil War. Regardless of where Jim Crow laws were passed, however, they had crippling social, political, and economic effects on black citizens. They frequently resulted in substandard public services for African Americans despite legislators' claims to the contrary.

As a rule, whites tended to have access to newer, cleaner, and more comfortable public facilities than blacks. For instance, schools for African American children generally featured run-down classrooms and outdated books. Public

Two men drink at segregated drinking fountains in the South.

rest rooms designated for "colored" use were frequently cramped, filthy, and without much privacy. Train cars that were set aside for black passengers were overcrowded and coated with coal dust—conditions that greatly contrasted with the spacious coach cars used by white riders.

Jim Crow laws also criminalized marriage between blacks and whites and placed restrictions on African Americans at the ballot box. Specifically, several southern states demanded that citizens pass literacy tests or pay poll taxes before they were allowed to vote. Since blacks often lacked educational and economic opportunities in the late 1800s and early 1900s, such requirements kept many of them away from the polls.

Nor were Jim Crow laws the only challenge African Americans faced during this period. The Ku Klux Klan (KKK), a secret society founded shortly after the end of the Civil War, and similar groups intimidated black communities throughout the South. Wearing white robes and hoods to conceal their identities, Klansmen quickly gained notoriety for their violent tactics. Members of the KKK frequently relied on arson and vandalism to intimidate black citizens from taking advantage of their constitutional rights. Klansmen also perpetuated terror by lynching their

African Americans were frequent targets of the KKK.

victims—burning, beating, shooting, or hanging them as a warning to any African Americans who dared to question or challenge racial inequality.

Nevertheless, even in the face of humiliation and terror, blacks demonstrated that they were growing increasingly tired of giving in. From waging legal battles against segregation to forming civil rights organizations, African Americans began shaping a remarkable legacy of activism in the late nineteenth and early twentieth centuries.

Landmark Legal Cases and Early Activism

Neither the KKK nor decades of post–Civil War discrimination could stop the mounting desire for change that had sprung up in black communities across the nation as the 1800s drew to a close. Homer Plessy was living evidence of this fact. In June 1892 Plessy, an African American, boarded a car designated for the exclusive use of white passengers on the East Louisiana Railroad. Conductors ordered him to relocate to a seating area set aside for black riders, but he refused and was subsequently imprisoned for breaking state segregation laws.

When arguing his case before John Ferguson, a local district court judge, Plessy insisted that the rights guaranteed to him in the Fourteenth Amendment had been violated by the East Louisiana Railroad. Ferguson said that Louisiana had the authority to regulate its railroads as it saw fit—including according to the principles of segregation—within state lines. Plessy responded to the judge's guilty verdict by filing suit against him.

By 1896 attorneys on either side of *Plessy v. Ferguson* were debating the issue of segregation before the Supreme Court.

Ultimately, however, a majority of Supreme Court justices, deciding in favor of Ferguson, lent their support to what became known as the "separate but equal" doctrine. In their ruling, the justices said that segregation was legal so long as blacks were provided with public services and facilities that were essentially equal to those offered to whites. "We consider the underlying fallacy of the plaintiff's argument to consist in the assumption that the enforced separation of the two races stamps the colored race with a badge of inferiority," wrote Justice Henry Billings Brown. "The argument also assumes that social prejudices may be overcome by legislation, and that equal rights cannot be secured to the Negro except by an enforced commingling of the two races."

Though the Supreme Court decision was undeniably a blow to African American citizens, black activists continued to push for social and political changes. They believed that doing otherwise amounted to passively accepting segregation and its destructive side effects. For those who were eager to intimidate African Americans who stood up for their constitutional rights, *Plessy v. Ferguson* had rendered such blacks more defenseless than ever.

In February 1909 W. E. B. Du Bois, Joel Spingarn, William Monroe Trotter, John Hope, Jane Addams, Mary White Ovington, and other civil rights pioneers formed the National Association for the Advancement of Colored People (NAACP). Both African Americans and whites who wanted to end segregation joined this group. The NAACP vowed

> to promote equality of rights and eradicate caste or race prejudice among citizens of the United States; to advance the interest of

> colored citizens; to secure for them impartial suffrage; and to increase their opportunities for securing justice in the courts, education for their children, employment according to their ability, and complete equality before the law.

To accomplish these goals, NAACP members waged a series of legal battles within America's court system. For example, activists pushed for tougher punishments for criminals found guilty of committing racial violence. They also called for an end to segregation in settings ranging from law schools to voting booths.

In addition, Thurgood Marshall, the future Supreme Court justice, and other NAACP leaders created the organization's Legal Defense and Educational Fund (LDF) in 1940 to provide legal aid to blacks struggling with poverty and oppression. Over the next decade, new civil rights groups, including the Women's Political Council (WPC), took root as well. Like the NAACP, the WPC and similar organizations encouraged African Americans to fight discriminatory voting practices, bus segregation, and other injustices that impacted on their lives and constitutional freedoms.

As the efforts of civil rights activists intensified, so did national debate surrounding whether or not the United States should be shaped by the "separate but equal" doctrine. This doctrine was called into question in part because there was rarely any true equality between the services and facilities set aside for whites and those designated for blacks. Lawyers with the LDF emphasized this fact when they argued the landmark Supreme Court case *Brown v. Board of Education* in the early 1950s.

The now famous legal battle originally began when thirteen African American parents in Topeka, Kansas, fought the local school board over what they considered unfair treatment of their children. These parents complained that black students were denied enrollment in the closest neighborhood schools and were instead forced to travel excessive distances in order to attend segregated facilities. At the time, African American parents in other parts of the country—including Washington, DC; Delaware; South Carolina; and Virginia—voiced similar concerns about their children's educational opportunities.

Eventually, LDF attorneys, including Marshall, presented their arguments to the Supreme Court. The justices who handed down the decision in *Brown v. Board of Education* in May 1954 did not safeguard segregation. In fact, their decision reversed the "separate but equal" doctrine of Plessy.

As Chief Justice Earl Warren declared in a unanimous decision, "We conclude that, in the field of public education, the doctrine of 'separate but equal' has no place. Separate educational facilities are inherently unequal." Though the Supreme Court verdict was a victory for Marshall and his fellow civil rights activists, not everyone immediately respected it. Many southern schools continued to be segregated. Nor was the classroom the only setting where segregation continued. As an upcoming boycott in Montgomery would soon reinforce, public buses were another.

Two
Beginnings of the Boycott

Jim Crow laws and other forms of discrimination posed multiple problems for African Americans during the 1950s. Their impact on public transportation in the South was especially felt because many blacks who resided in Montgomery, Alabama, and other southern cities generally relied on buses to take them to and from work. For many poor black families, owning a car was an unaffordable luxury.

Complicating matters was the fact that segregation frequently limited the availability of public services and facilities in black communities. Employment and educational opportunities in these areas were also generally lacking. It was therefore not uncommon for African Americans to travel several miles each day in order to attend work or school. Walking was obviously not always a practical solution; so some blacks carpooled with whichever of their friends, family, or neighbors had access to an automobile. An alternative mode of transportation was bus companies, such as the Montgomery City Lines, which abided by municipal laws that supported segregated seating.

Despite the inconveniences and humiliation routinely experienced by blacks on city buses, they often had no other choice and so continued to ride them. In fact, historians estimate that anywhere from 66 to 75 percent of the men and women who boarded the Montgomery City Lines in the early 1950s were African American. As several civil rights activists were well aware, Rosa Parks was not the first of them to challenge the authority of the company's all-white staff.

By the time Parks took her famous ride, organizations such as the NAACP and the WPC had already spent several years trying to reform bus segregation laws. These groups urged Montgomery lawmakers and the Montgomery City Lines to model their rules regarding segregated seating after those that already existed in Mobile, Alabama. While black passengers in Mobile were expected to sit in a separate portion of the bus, they were not obligated to give up their seats to accommodate white riders.

In the early 1950s, activists in the NAACP, the WPC, and similar organizations saw Mobile's approach as a suitable—if not ideal—answer to some of the challenges faced by African Americans who rode Montgomery buses. Many believed that it was impractical to try to persuade city officials to totally eliminate segregation laws related to public transportation. Leaders of local civil rights groups recognized that policies promoting "separate but equal" treatment of blacks and whites were widely accepted in much of the South. While completely eliminating segregation on buses was a worthy goal, activists understood that a more reasonable ambition was to limit the ways in which it negatively impacted upon African Americans.

However, city officials and the Montgomery City Lines resisted any changes to the established system of segregated seating. In fact, local politicians had refused a request made by WPC representatives in the early 1950s to revise segregation laws to more closely resemble Mobile's policies. Yet African American leaders in Montgomery had only to look to civil rights activists in nearby Louisiana for inspiration about what tactics to use next.

In the spring of 1953, black residents in Baton Rouge, Louisiana, staged a bus boycott to protest Louisiana attorney general Fred LeBlanc's handling of local segregation laws. That March, LeBlanc had overturned an ordinance that permitted African Americans to take whatever seats were available when they rode local buses. According to this rule, though black passengers were still required to fill the seats from the rear of the vehicle before they took spots near the front, they faced few additional restrictions.

Though bus drivers had paid little attention to the ordinance and continued to harass African American riders, LeBlanc's reversal of the law formally legalized such behavior. Civil rights activists in Baton Rouge responded by boycotting the city's bus system. For approximately one week, they organized car pools for members of the black community who usually used public transportation. The boycott ended when the city council conceded that a policy of first-come, first-served seating would be reinstated. Officials also noted, however, that a few seats at the front of the bus would be reserved for white passengers and a few seats in the back for African American passengers.

While the boycott did not end segregated public transportation, it succeeded in improving how black riders in Baton Rouge were treated. Edgar Daniel "E. D." Nixon, leader of the Alabama chapter of the NAACP, was among several civil rights activists in Montgomery who waited for a similar opportunity to present itself in his city. Nixon also headed Montgomery's Brotherhood of Sleeping Car Porters—or the Pullman porters' union. Pullman porters were railroad employees who attended to passengers on a train's sleeping cars. A large number of these men were African American and so witnessed firsthand the segregation in public transportation.

By 1955 Nixon's focus was on buses, not trains. Together with Jo Ann Robinson, the WPC president, he was eager to change segregation laws affecting the Montgomery City Lines. Nixon's plan was to publicly protest the discrimination black passengers faced and to attack the legality of city policies that reinforced discrimination. Despite his confidence in this strategy, however, he realized that it would take time and careful planning to execute.

Planning the Protest

Nixon's task was not an easy one. First, he had to find the right person to challenge the Montgomery bus system's segregated seating policy. To this end, he looked for a local citizen who had been imprisoned or fined by authorities for standing up to discrimination on public transportation.

It was essential for such a person to be well respected and to possess character traits that would encourage the African American community to actively support a boycott. In addition, he or she had to be capable of enduring the rigors of serving as a plaintiff in a test case that would cause lawmakers to reconsider the city's segregation ordinances. Throughout 1955 a handful of black riders clashed with bus drivers and Montgomery police when they refused to give up their seats to accommodate white passengers. Yet Nixon did not find an ideal candidate among them.

Nixon already knew Rosa Parks before she distinguished herself on December 1, 1955. A longtime member of the Montgomery branch of the NAACP, Parks had been elected the group's secretary in 1943 and had actively participated in campaigns that encouraged African Americans to register to vote. In addition, she volunteered as the organization's youth council adviser and had attended training sessions in civil rights activism at a cultural center in Tennessee called the Highlander Folk School.

While Parks had not intended to become the face of African American opposition to bus segregation, she was far from politically naive. She did not shy away from controversy, as was made evident by her campaigning in behalf of Jeremiah Reeves, a young black Alabaman who faced execution for allegedly raping a white woman in the early 1950s. Many African Americans—including Parks—felt the case lacked foundation and that the death penalty was an overly severe punishment and rooted in racism rather than justice. Although Reeves was electrocuted in 1958, Parks's activism in his behalf demonstrated her awareness of civil rights issues and her willingness to stand up for her beliefs.

With Parks's arrest in 1955, Nixon seized the opportunity to launch a formal protest of segregated seating policies on city buses. As word of the imprisonment of this admired member of the community spread throughout Montgomery, black residents' frustration and anger intensified, and Nixon knew that the moment was finally right to take action.

On December 2, 1955, Nixon and Clifford Durr, a well-known Alabama attorney and white civil rights activist, headed to the city jail to post Parks's $100 bail. Durr's wife, Virginia, accompanied them. In addition to working at a local department store, Parks was also periodically employed by the Durrs as a seamstress.

Shortly after securing Parks's release, Nixon collaborated with Robinson on how to proceed next. They discussed the situation with Parks's lawyer, Fred D. Gray, who had established a name for himself as a civil rights activist. Twenty-four hours after Rosa Parks had refused to give up her seat on a Montgomery bus, a large-scale boycott of the city's bus system was being organized.

Robinson, an English professor at Alabama State College in Montgomery, worked feverishly with other WPC members to draft leaflets announcing the protest and calling upon concerned citizens to participate. These women toiled long after midnight and used the school's mimeograph to produce approximately 35,000 handbills. (A mimeograph is a type of printing press that was popular prior to the creation of photocopiers and that operates by forcing ink through a typed stencil.) The flier read as follows:

> This is for Monday, December 5, 1955.
> Another Negro woman has been arrested and thrown into jail because she refused to get up out of her seat on the bus for a white person to sit down. . . . This has to be stopped. Negroes have rights too, for if Negroes did not ride the buses, they could not operate. Three-fourths of the riders are Negroes, yet we are arrested, or have to stand behind empty seats. If you do not do something to stop those arrests, they will continue. The next time it may be you, or your daughter or

E. D. Nixon (center) and attorney Fred Gray (right) accompany Rosa Parks to court as she makes bond after her arrest.

> your mother. This woman's case will come up on Monday. We are, therefore, asking every Negro to stay off the buses Monday in protest of the arrest and trial. Don't ride the buses to work, to town, to school, or anywhere on Monday. . . . If you work, take a cab or walk. But please, children and grownups, don't ride the bus at all on Monday. Please stay off of all buses, Monday.

The following day, activists circulated the handbill throughout Montgomery's African American community. They distributed the flier at churches, private residences, restaurants, and stores. In the meantime, local civil rights leaders had gathered over the weekend to determine the logistics of the boycott. About 40,000 black passengers relied on the city's public buses for transportation. The majority of these men and women supported the principles behind the boycott but feared what their white employers would say when they failed to show up for work on Monday.

Community leaders promoted alternative modes of transportation, including organized neighborhood car pools. Citizens were also made aware of special rates being offered by Montgomery's eighteen African American–owned taxi companies, which agreed to charge only 10 cents a ride—approximately the same as the standard bus fare—on Monday.

Montgomery's Baptist ministers played an especially important role in the boycott efforts. Ralph Abernathy and Martin Luther King Jr. were among several local clergymen who endorsed the protest in their Sunday sermons and who met with NAACP and WPC members to finalize goals

Ralph Abernathy (left) and Martin Luther King Jr. (right) were active in the Montgomery boycott.

and strategies. They and other activists waited anxiously to see exactly how many African Americans would board city buses on Monday.

December 5, 1955

On December 5, 1955, a cold, windy, rainy day in Montgomery, 90 percent of black residents who normally used public

Black citizens walk to work and school as part of their boycott of Montgomery buses.

transportation found other ways to travel that day. Some rode mules or bicycles or got to work in horse-drawn buggies. Others took advantage of the car pools or the special rates being offered by local cab companies. Many citizens chose to walk—regardless of the inclement weather—to demonstrate their opposition to bus segregation laws.

Meanwhile, a crowd of hundreds of African Americans

Rosa Parks is escorted by E. D. Nixon to court, where she was subsequently ordered to pay a total of $14 in fines and court fees for her earlier arrest.

waited outside the courthouse where Parks was being tried by Judge John Scott. The trial lasted approximately half an hour and concluded with her conviction on charges of disorderly conduct and violating Montgomery's segregation ordinances.

Scott ordered Parks to pay a $10 fine and $4 in court costs. On the advice of Gray, she planned to formally appeal the judge's decision. In doing so, she challenged the validity of local segregation laws.

On the evening following Parks's trial and the first day of the bus boycott, black community leaders met once again. They gathered at Mount Zion African Methodist Episcopal (AME) Zion Church to determine whether the protest should be continued and, if so, the most practical and effective ways of extending it. Recognizing that tens of thousands of black citizens required bus service to get to school and work each day, activists had to come up with a long-term plan for alternative transportation. They also perceived the importance of forming an official group dedicated to providing the boycott with organization, financial support, and much-needed publicity.

Consequently, the black leaders who met on the evening of December 5 established the Montgomery Improvement Association (MIA). King, who was nominated the group's president, later explained that the purpose of the MIA was "to improve the general status of Montgomery, to improve race relations, and to uplift the general tenor of the community." However, the organization's most immediate ambition in late 1955 was to devise methods of maintaining the bus boycott.

Though King was only twenty-six years old and had resided in Montgomery for a relatively short period, activists believed him to be the best man to carry out this task. Unlike other local African American leaders, he had not had time to develop tense relationships with white officials over the city's segregation policies. More seasoned Montgomery

President of the MIA

King would one day be recognized as one of the most determined leaders of America's civil rights movement. In late 1955, however, he was a young husband and father, not to mention a relatively new resident of Montgomery. As a result, his initial reaction to being asked to serve as president of the MIA was understandable hesitancy.

"When he heard me talk about how long it'd take and how hard the struggle would be, he wasn't sure," Nixon later remembered. "He was a young man just getting started in the ministry. His family was young. His wife had given birth to their first child. . . . He said, 'Let me think about it a while and call me back.' After some more calls, I . . . told him straight out that I thought he was the man who should lead this thing.

He paced the floor a time or two, then he turned to me and said in that strong and powerful voice of his . . . 'Brother Nixon, if you think I'm the one, I'll do it.' I nodded and clasped his hand and held it, and I swear there was something stronger than ever in that handshake. I knew we'd all be one together."

activists reasoned that, in addition to being intelligent and well spoken, King was likely to have few enemies at the onset of the boycott.

After the MIA had been officially created, community leaders decided to hold a meeting at Montgomery's Holt Street Baptist Church to further discuss the boycott with local black citizens. Thousands of men, women, and children attended the gathering and voiced their ongoing support of the protest. Many were particularly moved to continue their activism when they were told of the formation of the MIA and subsequently heard King speak.

"There comes a time when people get tired," King explained to the throngs of African Americans who had made their way to the church that night. "We are here this evening to say to those who have mistreated us so long that we are tired—tired of being segregated and humiliated, tired of being kicked about by the brutal feet of oppression. . . . We had no alternative but to protest. If you will protest courageously, and yet with dignity . . . when the history books are written in future generations, the historians will have to pause and say, 'There lived a great people—a black people—who injected new meaning and dignity into the veins of civilization.'"

Like Parks and the tens of thousands of African Americans who lived and worked in Montgomery, King, too, was tired of accepting segregation and all the social injustices that accompanied it. Yet it is doubtful how many of these individuals could have guessed how long the bus boycott would last or what actual changes it would bring forth. As the days ahead revealed, varying perspectives shaped how the activists perceived what the goals of the protest should be.

The Reverend Martin Luther King Jr. discusses the boycott with a crowd of Montgomery citizens gathered at the Holt Street Baptist Church.

Different vantage points also divided the African American community on the role and effectiveness of filing a federal lawsuit to challenge the legality of segregation statutes.

Ultimately, the boycott drew nationwide attention and threw a spotlight on the realities of segregation and how it was viewed in America. In the end, as King correctly predicted, future historians would indeed pause when recollecting the chain of events that was set into motion in Montgomery in early December 1955.

Three
Protestors' Perspectives

FROM THE DAY IT BEGAN, the Montgomery Bus Boycott presented enormous challenges and risks for everyone from civil rights leaders to the average citizens who boycotted public transportation. Participants had to find alternative means of getting to school and work on time. Though many African Americans supported the ideas behind the protest, few could afford to sacrifice their incomes or their opportunities for an education.

Nor could such individuals ignore the potential threat to their physical safety that went hand in hand with civil rights activism. At that time, Montgomery, Alabama—like so much of the South—operated according to legal and social boundaries that revolved around segregation. Black residents who openly defied the accepted order of things inevitably invited the attention of the Ku Klux Klan (KKK) and other hate groups. Rosa Parks's husband, Raymond Parks, reminded his wife of this fact when E. D. Nixon and Clifford Durr first suggested that she use her court case to test the constitutionality of segregation laws.

Yet, despite his warning that "the white folks will kill you," Parks accepted the challenge to position herself at the forefront of the local protest. A common opinion at the onset of the boycott was that it would not last long and that it would not accomplish any dramatic form of racial integration. Martin Luther King Jr. and other activists in the MIA initially hoped that they could reach some sort of compromise with bus and city officials regarding segregated seating policies.

The specific list of demands that they wanted to see fulfilled were "courteous treatment on the buses; first-come, first-served seating, with whites in the front and blacks in the back; [and] hiring of black drivers for the black bus routes." Further, activists requested that no African American riders be forced to give up their seat or stand over an empty seat. King, Robinson, Gray, and Abernathy expressed these goals at meetings they arranged with city leaders and representatives of the Montgomery City Lines shortly after the boycott began. Nixon regularly communicated with MIA members but was frequently absent from meetings because of his responsibilities with the Pullman porters' union.

During the early stages of the boycott, civil rights activists were primarily pushing for the improved treatment of black passengers. The goal of complete integration of Montgomery's buses was not considered a realistic ambition. Such was the attitude of MIA spokesmen when they met with Mayor William Gayle, Police Commissioner Clyde Sellers, Public Works Commissioner Frank Parks, and Jack Crenshaw, an attorney who represented the Montgomery City Lines, at City Hall on December 8, 1955. Both print and television reporters were present during the discussion.

"Surely the world will see that our demands are not out of line," noted Abernathy. "Perhaps they will see what we're facing." King likewise stated that he and other MIA

Martin Luther King Jr. outlines strategies for the bus boycott with his fellow activists.

members merely sought "reforms of existing rules and regulations." City and bus company officials, however, were not convinced that activists were proposing simple requests.

Despite King's promise that Montgomery's African American residents would not use violence to achieve their goals and that the boycott would end as soon as their demands were met, Gayle and his colleagues hesitated. These men said they would attempt to ensure that black passengers were treated courteously but insisted that altering seating arrangements would violate local segregation laws. They also emphasized that they had no intention of hiring African American drivers, regardless of how many black riders patronized the Montgomery City Lines.

As December 1955 wore on, MIA representatives and city and bus officials remained deadlocked. Gayle appointed a special biracial committee that was intended to facilitate a compromise between both groups, but no agreement was reached as 1955 drew to a close. As the boycott continued, opinions within the MIA and Montgomery's African American community began to shift—both in regard to how to produce the most change and what goals the protest should ideally accomplish.

The Price of Opposing Segregation

As the weeks passed in December, the stakes of challenging the city's bus segregation laws grew higher. There were increasing outbursts of violence and vandalism. Bus drivers reported that their vehicles were peppered with gunfire when they drove through African American neighborhoods. Meanwhile, Montgomery's black residents stated that they were repeatedly threatened with physical violence by white citizens.

Though Gayle and his colleagues did not publicly condone such actions, neither did they do much to reach a compromise with the MIA. In fact, the mayor appeared to be taking a tougher stand against boycotters as 1955 concluded. Specifically, he urged white employers not to drive their African American workers to and from job sites.

In addition, local police frequently fined or arrested boycotters who waited to be picked up at car pool stops organized by the MIA. By mid–December 1955, the group had established a car pool system that eventually came to include more than two hundred cars and station wagons. Blacks relied heavily on this alternative mode of transportation. They had few other choices, especially once police started ordering taxi drivers to resume their normal rates and not offer protestors any reduced fares.

Yet the MIA-sponsored car pool had its share of troubles. Besides having to raise funds to purchase vehicles and fuel, activists were forced to deal with local authorities, who were known to ticket and imprison participating drivers for moving either too fast or too slow. They also harassed groups of African Americans who gathered at car pool stops; blacks were often accused, in most instances falsely, of loitering, damaging private property, or being public nuisances.

Nixon later noted that such treatment inevitably caused the resolve of black citizens who supported the boycott to be put to the test as time passed. He recalled that the initial days of the protest were filled with fervor and a ready willingness to make sacrifices in the name of reforming segregation. Yet enduring the challenges that subsequently arose was no easy task.

"Although we raised a lot of money in those first days and weeks, I knew we had to keep on organizing, tightening the nuts and bolts of our operation every day," Nixon observed. "And the preachers had their hands full, keeping the folks who were being threatened every day with violence or jail or the loss of their jobs from being worn down and giving up."

Meanwhile, the Montgomery City Lines experienced a sharp decline in business, with some company officials estimating about $400 in daily losses. By early January 1956,

A group of African Americans participate in a car pool during the bus boycott.

representatives of the bus service asked the city commission for permission to hike rates so as not to have to lay off drivers or cut routes. Gayle responded to the mounting financial and social crisis by becoming even more unwilling to negotiate with King and the MIA.

In mid–January, however, the mayor announced that a compromise had been reached with black protestors and that the boycott was at an end. Tensions between the MIA and Montgomery officials flared when King denied that any such agreement had been established. On the contrary, King said, Gayle had "hoodwinked" three of his colleagues—who wished to remain anonymous—into a secret meeting. King also accused the mayor of falsely declaring that both sides had come to amicable terms that would conclude the boycott.

With relations between the MIA and city and bus officials growing more strained by the day, it was clear that negotiations were at a standstill. In the meantime, the daily risks protestors took were becoming increasingly apparent. On January 26, 1956, King himself was pulled over by local police, who charged him with speeding and promptly jailed him. While officers ultimately acknowledged that he was going only about five miles an hour over the limit, the MIA leader was tried, found guilty of speeding, and fined $10 plus another $4 in court costs.

As King was receiving threatening phone calls from a mounting number of whites who opposed his efforts, he seriously considered abandoning his leadership of the MIA in the days following his arrest. King decided to forge ahead, but the decision was not easy and was made even more difficult when his home was bombed on the evening of January 30.

That night, someone tossed a bomb onto the front porch of his house while King was attending a meeting. His wife, Coretta, and their infant daughter, Yolanda, were inside with a family friend, but no one was harmed. Gayle, members of the Montgomery police, and several hundred African Americans gathered outside King's home shortly after King returned.

City officials promised that they were against such violence and vowed to find the culprits. King continued to urge members of the black community to remain calm and peaceful in the days ahead.

As one local journalist observed, however, "Those people were so angry, you could feel it. Tension was in the air. It was about to explode." With emotions becoming more heated and frustration with city officials building, it was time to contemplate a new approach to fighting bus segregation laws.

An Alternative to Compromise

The concept of a test case that would challenge the constitutionality of bus segregation laws was not new to the MIA. Activists including Gray and Nixon had contemplated the notion for some time. Yet, in order to avoid the intensive preparation for a long-term legal battle, the MIA hoped instead to compromise with local officials and the Montgomery City Lines.

As Gale's stubbornness grew more apparent, however, the need for an alternative approach also became obvious. The mounting harassment and violence directed at boycotters also compelled MIA leaders to reconsider their objectives. After consulting with Nixon and Durr and two renowned African American attorneys, Thurgood Marshall and Robert Carter, Gray urged the organization to support him in filing a lawsuit.

He explained that the case would be rooted in the argument that the treatment of black passengers who rode the Montgomery City Lines was a violation of their constitutional rights. Specifically, Gray insisted that bus segregation laws contradicted the due process and equal protection clauses guaranteed to U.S. citizens by the Fourteenth Amendment, commonly referred to as the Civil Rights Amendment. The amendment states,

> All persons born or naturalized in the United States and subject to the jurisdiction thereof, are citizens of the United States and of the state wherein they reside. No state shall make or enforce any law which shall abridge the privileges or immunities of citizens of the United States; nor shall any state deprive any person of life, liberty, or property, without due process of law; nor deny to any person within its jurisdiction the equal protection of the laws.

The amendment essentially promises that, in ensuring due process, the government is obligated to treat all citizens fairly by maintaining certain rules and standards that protect Americans' various freedoms. In addition, it emphasizes that individual states are also required to grant their residents equal protection under the law. Gray contended that segregated seating aboard Montgomery buses and the discrimination African Americans faced when they objected to it were in direct violation of these rights. MIA leaders agreed and, by the end of January 1956, were prepared to publicly support a lawsuit based on Gray's arguments.

Gray and a local attorney named Charles Langford filed the case on February 1, 1956, in Alabama's federal district court. Though it came as a surprise to some individuals who were familiar with the Montgomery Bus Boycott, lawyers

The Cases of Claudette Colvin and Mary Louise Smith

Shortly before Parks's arrest, Nixon had considered two other Montgomery City Lines passengers as possible key players in a local fight against bus segregation laws. In March 1955 fifteen-year-old Claudette Colvin had refused to give up her seat to a white rider and was subsequently arrested. Nixon was at first confident that he could use the teenager's case to oppose bus segregation policies. When he later discovered that she was pregnant, he worried that Colvin's social status as a young unwed mother would be a distraction from the primary issues at hand. Nixon recognized that anyone whom he and local black leaders relied upon to win widespread public support of a bus boycott needed to be morally unquestionable.

The following October Nixon had fleeting hopes that a second teenager, Mary Louise Smith, might meet such requirements. Like Colvin, Smith was arrested for objecting to giving up her seat on a Montgomery bus. Smith's father, however, insisted that she plead guilty and pay whatever fines were necessary to facilitate a quick and quiet end to the matter. She and Colvin therefore could not be considered for the focal point of any protest. In March 1956, however, the two young women agreed to be named as plaintiffs in *Browder v. Gayle* and thus played important roles in another legal case protesting bus segregation laws.

decided not to name Parks as a plaintiff in the lawsuit. Parks was in the midst of an ongoing criminal case that stemmed from her alleged violation of bus segregation laws the previous December. Attorneys did not want the civil suit they filed in February 1956 to stall because of any legal preoccupation with these charges. While they were eager to see the courts act in Parks's favor, they needed their efforts to culminate in far more than a dismissal of her individual case.

As Gray explained, he "wanted the court to have only one issue to decide—the constitutionality of the laws requiring segregation on the buses." So he and Langford selected four other African Americans who had experienced discrimination on the Montgomery City Lines. In 1955 Mary Louise Smith, Claudette Colvin, Aurelia Browder, and Susie McDonald had all had experiences that were not unlike Parks's.

Each of these women agreed to be part of the civil suit that became known as *Browder v. Gayle*. The defendants named in the case were Mayor Gayle, Commissioners Sellers and Parks, Montgomery Chief of Police Goodwin Ruppenthal, and the Montgomery City Lines and two of its drivers, James Blake and Robert Cleere. C. C. "Jack" Owen, Jimmy Hitchcock, and Sibyl Pool—all members of the Alabama Public Service Commission—were listed on the suit, as well.

The stage was set for a fight that would reshape Americans' ideas about and acceptance of segregation. It was not that civil rights activists had suddenly altered their objectives or ambitions. King had already expressed his desire to completely overturn segregation when he witnessed the reluctance of city and bus officials to compromise on issues surrounding the boycott.

"Frankly, I am for immediate integration," he told a reporter in January 1956. "Segregation is evil, and I cannot, as a minister, condone evil." When the suit was actually filed, however, the court was asked to declare bus segregation laws unconstitutional. Their efforts were complicated by the fact that not everyone shared their point of view.

Four
Common White Counterpoints

A GREAT DEAL TRANSPIRED in the two weeks after Fred Gray and Charles Langford filed *Browder v. Gayle* in a federal district court. Violence against residents who supported the Montgomery Bus Boycott continued to intensify. In early February 1956 E. D. Nixon's home was bombed. No one was injured. In addition, area police kept up their harassment of protest leaders and participants in the citywide car pool. They ticketed, fined, and arrested these individuals on a variety of misdemeanor charges such as vehicular speeding.

As of mid–February 1956 local officials were also investigating whether or not they could level more relevant accusations of legal wrongdoing at members of the MIA. By February 21, 1956, attorneys representing the city and acting with the encouragement and support of Mayor Gayle and his subordinates decided that they could indeed file new charges against African American activists. That day, a Montgomery County grand jury indicted approximately 115 key protestors on the grounds that they had violated a statute that prohibited staging boycotts without just cause.

Nixon, King, Parks, Robinson, and Abernathy were among the accused. In most cases, they posted bond and

A crowd gathers outside the Montgomery County Courthouse. Many of these men and women were arraigned for their involvement in the boycott.

were subsequently released from the city jail. Though supporters of the boycott perceived the incident as yet one more example of persecution of civil rights leaders, the mayor and Montgomery officials took another perspective. Any activism that promoted the limitation or end of segregation laws was a threat to stability, peace, and a well-accepted social order in their city.

In Gayle's opinion, the boycott was essentially being orchestrated by a handful of troublemakers "who have split asunder the fine relationships which have existed between the Negro and white people for generations." He further emphasized that these men and women were intent on wrecking "the social fabric of our community." Gayle and a majority of Montgomery officials spoke out against the violence that Nixon, King, and other MIA leaders had been subjected to. At the same time, however, they viewed such episodes as examples of the upheaval and chaos that must be expected when local segregation was challenged.

The perspective of city leaders did not take into account the humiliation, inconveniences, and overall demoralization that African Americans suffered as a result of segregated seating and laws that sponsored similar discrimination. Gayle and men like him lived in a part of the South that, since the conclusion of the Civil War, was defined by detailed legal codes that kept blacks separate from whites. Montgomery officials feared the changes and general loss of control they would experience if these laws were watered down or overturned. They worried that day-to-day life would be drastically altered on countless social, economic, and political fronts. As the boycott continued, some of Montgomery's white residents expressed this sentiment differently.

"This bunch of niggers aren't going to rule this city," Police Commissioner Clyde Sellers reportedly remarked to some of his colleagues at City Hall in regard to MIA leaders. "We're gonna watch 'em like hawks. They'll break the law, and we'll swoop down and put 'em behind bars. . . . There's a lot of mad white people all over town who are not going to stand for this mess. I tell you, we better not give 'em an inch."

Standing Up for the Southern Way of Life

Sellers was not exaggerating about the numbers of angry white citizens who stood in staunch opposition to the Montgomery Bus Boycott. On February 10, 1956, thousands of these men and women applauded city leaders during a meeting of the local chapter of the White Citizens' Council (WCC). This organization—which was founded in 1954 and claimed tens of thousands of supporters throughout the South—believed that boycotters were a direct threat to their "Southern way of life."

Unlike the Ku Klux Klan, the WCC generally did not admit to using violence or terror tactics to demonstrate its opposition to integration. Though both groups shared strong ties, the WCC was regarded as a more upstanding and socially acceptable organization. Members of the WCC met in public and frequently relied upon legal or economic tactics to harass civil rights activists.

For instance, in December 1955 leaders of the group's Montgomery branch had pressured local insurance agencies into refusing coverage to black vehicle owners who were participating in the MIA-sponsored car pool. In response, several of the African American churches that had purchased many of the cars in question turned to the famous British insurer Lloyd's of London, which granted them new policies. Yet winning this small victory was only half the battle for boycotters, as they still had to deal repeatedly with other examples of opposition from both the WCC and the KKK.

In addition, some activists believed that city and bus officials regularly collaborated with the WCC and the KKK throughout the winter of 1956. While Mayor Gayle and his colleagues spoke out against the bombings of the homes of MIA members, they still had much in common with members of these organizations. Rethinking the segregation policy of the Montgomery City Lines—or segregation in any context for that matter—was unacceptable to them.

Public support of the WCC became obvious just two months after the bus boycott began, when the organization claimed its membership had doubled. Gayle was among those Montgomery citizens who joined the group's ranks following the start of the protest. His explanation as to why he decided to become a member shows how much he had in common with other white southerners who feared a loss of social, political, and economic control.

"I think every right-thinking white person in Montgomery, Alabama and the South should do the same," Gayle declared after joining the WCC. "We must make certain that Negroes are not allowed to force their demands on us." This point of view was cited time and again by the city's white working-class population. Terry Leon Hall, a local service station employee who admitted involvement in the bombings that targeted MIA leaders, used it as an excuse for his actions.

"Like Mayor Gayle said, the niggers were trying to destroy our way of life," he later recalled. "And we liked the way we had been living. . . . Up to that time, I'd never done a thing to a Negro. But I was hot and tired. I wasn't gonna stand for them to keep on doing this thing they called a boycott. What the hell, it was un-American!" From Hall's perspective, any violence he committed was done in the name of preserving southern society as he had come to understand and appreciate it. Sam Engelhardt, an Alabama state senator and a known white supremacist leader, preached almost identical ideals to 20,000 Montgomery citizens attending a WCC meeting in early 1956, saying:

> The niggers are getting out of control. They think they can do anything they want. They think they are just as good as me and you. Well, we know damn well they aren't . . . . They think just because one little ol' pinheaded nigger said "no" to a bus driver they can do anything they want to do. They think just because one nigger leader [named] Martin Luther King stands up in front of 'em and waves his black hand they can march down the street without being run over. Well, I'm here to tell you we got to drive straight and steady. We got to make sure they don't take over the streets—or the schoolhouses—or the city buses.

Eager to See the Boycott End

A large number of Montgomery's white residents may have agreed with Engelhardt's perspective, but others were feeling the economic effects of vacant seats on city buses. James Bagley, the Montgomery City Lines transportation superintendent, estimated in early 1956 that the company was losing approximately $12,000 a month. He calculated that it cost between 40 and 44 cents a mile to operate a bus; this figure included expenses such as gas and the driver's salary. Since the boycott had begun, Bagley estimated that the Montgomery City Lines had lost an average of 22 cents for every mile

Two white women are the only riders on this Montgomery bus during the boycott.

of service. He was also quick to add that his numbers were probably on the low side.

To compensate for the financial losses the boycott was causing, the bus company hiked fares for its remaining riders—most of whom were white. Yet the economic impact of the protest stretched even further than passengers' pocketbooks. Since African Americans were often without alternative modes of transportation, they shopped less often outside their immediate neighborhoods. As a result, store owners in downtown Montgomery and several nearby areas felt a strain on their businesses as well.

In response, some tried to negotiate directly with the MIA. These businessmen even formed a group known as the Men of Montgomery in an attempt to speed up negotiations with African American activists. They agreed to the majority of the demands that the MIA had made when it first attempted to reach a compromise on segregated seating with city officials and representatives of the Montgomery City Lines. As of late February 1956, though, the Men of Montgomery had failed to offer boycotters a settlement that promised to fully integrate local buses.

By that time, Gray and Langford were already using *Browder v. Gayle* to question the legality of segregated public transportation. Consequently, the unwillingness of local business leaders to more fully support total integration of city buses was a deal breaker in negotiations between the Men of Montgomery and the MIA. The point of the Men of Montgomery's efforts was to restore financial security—not to end segregation. MIA activists obviously had different goals in mind, and they therefore rejected the final settlement offer made by the Men of Montgomery on February 20, 1956.

Meanwhile, like the city's prominent businessmen, many of Montgomery's other white residents were forced to weigh their support of segregation against the disruption the boycott was causing to their lives. For example, Mayor Gayle had urged white housewives to stop giving their black maids and cooks rides to and from work each day. He advised them and any citizens who aided African American protestors that they were making themselves the subject of ridicule by unwittingly promoting the boycott.

The Perspective of a White MIA Member

While an overwhelming number of Montgomery's white residents opposed the boycott or at least expressed some hesitancy about integrating buses, there were a few notable exceptions to this rule. Robert Graetz (center right) was one of them. The local Lutheran minister was a prominent member of the MIA and openly supported an end to bus segregation laws. As a result of his views, Graetz and his family were frequently the targets of vandalism and attempted violence. At one point, he was even arrested by Montgomery police, who used his participation in the MIA-sponsored car pool to charge him with "illegally running a taxi service."

"People either loved us or hated us," Graetz recalled almost five decades after the boycott occurred. "Few showed indifference. People often said we had courage. There were times when I was scared to death." Graetz never abandoned his

support of the boycott, which he later described as a pivotal moment in the civil rights movement.

"The bus boycott, you have to remember, was the beginning of the modern Civil Rights movement. Once the boycott started here, it spread to other cities. It encouraged people to get involved in other ways in dealing with other aspects of segregation and discrimination."

"The Negroes are laughing at white people behind their backs," Gayle remarked. "They think it's very funny and amusing that whites who are opposed to the Negro boycott will act as chauffeurs to Negroes who are boycotting the buses." He also observed, "The Negroes have made their own bed, and the whites should let them sleep in it." For several of Montgomery's white residents, however, this was easier said than done as the boycott wore on.

From the viewpoint of men and women who relied upon black housekeepers, nannies, and cooks, the protest was forcing their employees to show up late or sometimes miss work altogether. While Montgomery's more affluent white citizens often favored segregation, the cost of taking a firm stand against the boycott was impacting the tranquillity and organization they valued in their home lives. In addition, local police commissioners had spread word that African American gangs, or goon squads, were using violence and intimidation to keep black passengers off buses.

City officials had hoped that promoting this idea would make residents believe that only a handful of disgruntled activists were behind the boycott. They wanted the public to feel that most black citizens did not have a problem with segregated seating policies on the Montgomery City Lines. As they soon discovered, though, their strategy partially backfired. Some of the white housewives who drove their employees to and from work claimed they did so to "protect them from [the] harassment" of the African American goon squads that police had spread the word about.

By March 1956 this was merely one of many opinions that members of Montgomery's white community voiced in regard to issues related to the boycott. Yet it would not be long before public focus shifted to the federal judges. In May 1956 attorneys on either side of *Browder v. Gayle* began to present their arguments in court. As they did so, Americans across the nation watched and waited to see if judges would rule that segregated seating on city buses was a direct violation of the U.S. Constitution.

Five
Judicial Rulings and Public Reactions

Despite a significant amount of public anticipation surrounding *Browder v. Gayle,* the case did not officially get under way in Alabama's federal district court until May 11, 1956. In the weeks leading up to that date, however, a series of other events related to segregated public transportation made news headlines throughout much of the South. The first such event occurred on April 23, 1956, when the Supreme Court dismissed an appeal to overturn a South Carolina statute prohibiting bus segregation.

Within a day of the ruling, bus companies in more than a dozen major southern cities began reversing their seating policies in favor of racial integration. The Montgomery City Lines also started preparing to desegregate its vehicles. Mayor Gayle responded by ordering the company to obey local segregation laws and threatening drivers who failed to do so with arrest. He also asked a state court to issue an injunction commanding the Montgomery City Lines to comply with these statutes. The request was granted in early May 1956, but by then *Browder v. Gayle* was on the verge of being presented to a panel of three federal judges in Montgomery, Alabama.

On May 11, 1956, the plaintiffs' attorneys, Fred Gray, Charles Langford, and Robert Carter, filed into court prepared to demonstrate how local bus segregation laws violated the Fourteenth Amendment. Lawyers representing the city, including Walter Knabe and John Patterson, were ready to show how desegregating public transportation would inevitably lead to racial violence. Judges Richard Rives, Frank Johnson Jr., and Seybourn Lynne listened to attorneys' oral arguments and the testimony of numerous witnesses throughout most of May 1956. By early June the panel announced its ruling.

The judges' perspectives were shaped by many different factors, including decisions that had been handed down by the Supreme Court as far back as 1896 and as recently as 1954. On the one hand, *Plessy v. Ferguson* provided a legal defense for Jim Crow laws and "separate but equal" policies. On the other, *Brown v. Board of Education* had effectively rejected this concept by declaring that segregation had no place in public schools.

From the vantage point of Johnson and Rives, *Brown v. Board of Education* had set a legal precedent that impacted the situation at hand. They believed that since the Supreme Court had rejected the "separate but equal" doctrine, the same principle should be applied to segregated public transportation.

"As far as I'm concerned," Johnson observed to his colleagues on the panel, "state-imposed segregation on public facilities violates the Constitution. I'm going to rule with the plaintiffs here." From Lynne's perspective, *Brown* applied strictly to public schools while *Browder v. Gayle* dealt with public buses. Consequently, Lynne responded to Johnson's reasoning: "I don't reach it that way. As far as I'm concerned, the court has already spoken on this issue in *Plessy*. It's the law, and we're bound by it until it's changed." With Johnson and Rives choosing to decide for the plaintiffs, *Browder v. Gayle* ended in a ruling that declared bus segregation laws unconstitutional.

"We hold that the statutes and ordinances requiring segregation of the white and colored races on the motor buses of a common carrier of passengers in the city of Montgomery and its police jurisdiction . . . violate the due process and equal protection of the law . . . under the Fourteenth Amendment of the Constitution of the United States," the judges noted in their official written opinion, which was released on June 19, 1956. "The 'separate but equal' doctrine set forth by the Supreme Court in 1896 in the case of *Plessy v. Ferguson* can no longer be applied."

Opinions on the Ruling

Public reaction to the decision in *Browder v. Gayle* was varied in Montgomery and throughout much of the United States. Many white southerners especially were not happy with the federal court's ruling. Mayor Gayle announced that the city would appeal.

Meanwhile, attorneys for the plaintiffs in *Browder v. Gayle* and leaders of the MIA rejoiced at their legal triumph. Yet most recognized that their victory was far from complete. The judicial order that rendered the city's bus segregation laws unconstitutional was not likely to go into effect while an appeal to the Supreme Court remained pending. The fact that the case would not be presented to the Court until November 1956 meant that an entire summer of tension and uncertainty lay ahead for Montgomery residents.

The Price of Judgment

Judges Johnson and Rives found that their ruling on the boycott and bus segregation laws came at a price. Johnson reported that members of Montgomery's First Baptist Church refused to sit near his family when they attended Sunday services. For his part, however, the judge was determined not to be flustered by this reaction. "They may do their best to embarrass me," he observed, "but, as far as I'm concerned, they only embarrass themselves."

Like his colleague, Rives attempted to shrug off the responses of those white citizens who opposed his decision. Vandals desecrated his son's grave not long after the federal court issued its ruling. In addition, a local journalist wrote that Rives had "forfeited the right to be buried in Southern soil."

Gayle and other city officials, not content to sit idly by while awaiting the autumn court date, hit back at activists with whatever legal strategies they could. One such tactic involved questioning the ethics and business practices of members of the NAACP and trying to shut down the group's operations in Alabama.

In addition, local leaders prepared to file a lawsuit against car pool operators. Attorneys representing the city argued that these individuals had failed to obtain permission to use "the streets . . . for the construction or operation of any public utility." Their request for an injunction against the MIA-sponsored car pool was the subject of a court hearing that was scheduled for November 13, 1956.

In the meantime, as the boycott continued, activists remained targets of violence and harassment. Even whites who supported integration on city buses were at risk of violence. On August 25, 1956, the home of Robert Graetz, a white Lutheran minister and MIA member, was bombed (Graetz and his family were uninjured). Despite such incidents, many activists maintained the perspective that, even with an appeal to the Supreme Court pending, the boycott had changed African Americans' lives for the better.

"Through their unity, their carpools, their determination to share and share alike, they have found each other—as Negroes," observed a political science professor named J. E. Pierce of Montgomery's black residents. "[They] walk a little straighter . . . head a little higher. This new dignity is not accidental. And it is no accident that they call each other 'ladies' and 'gentlemen' on every possible occasion. For the first time in their lives, they feel like ladies and gentlemen from the bottom to the top."

By mid-November 1956, the Supreme Court handed down a ruling that further strengthened this sense of confidence. That autumn, the justices carefully considered the arguments of Patterson and Knabe as they appealed the decision of the federal district judges the previous June. They also listened to the reasoning of attorneys who believed that state and local laws supporting the segregation of Montgomery buses were unconstitutional. Carter, Gray, Langford, and Marshall made up the team of litigators who voiced this point of view before the Supreme Court.

On November 13, the Court declared its unanimous agreement with these men. The Court upheld the appellate court's ruling in *Browder v. Gayle*. In addition to referencing *Brown v. Board of Education*, the justices cited recent cases they had presided over in which they had outlawed segregation within public parks and golf courses.

Reboarding Montgomery's Buses

Back in Montgomery, word of the Supreme Court's ruling began to spread. King and other MIA leaders were in the process of defending their car pool efforts to Eugene Carter, a local circuit court judge, when they first heard news of their victory. They were overjoyed, but their enthusiasm was tempered.

Despite being informed of the ruling in *Browder*, Carter issued an injunction against the car pool. Further complicating matters were the realities of how and when the Court's ruling would be enforced in Montgomery. The process of desegregating buses would not go into effect until a formal notice outlining the justices' orders was sent to the city's federal district court. Issuing the notices would take several weeks.

Until then, the MIA announced that the boycott would continue, though King nevertheless described the ruling as "a glorious daybreak to end a long night of enforced segregation." Officials representing both Montgomery and the state of Alabama took a different perspective. These men insisted that they would ask the Supreme Court to reconsider the decision and, in the meantime, had no intention of altering bus segregation laws. Speaking on behalf of the White Citizens' Council (WCC), Sam Engelhardt encouraged Montgomery's white residents to continue their efforts to preserve a segregated society.

He added that if the Supreme Court "insists on disrupting our social order, including destroying the peaceful coexistence that has existed here for years, it must make preparations to enforce this order." However, the justices refused to hear further appeals. On December 17, 1956, they announced that they would not alter their judgment, and three days later official notice of the Supreme Court decision arrived in Montgomery.

That same day, the MIA voted to end the bus boycott. After more than a year of refusing to patronize the Montgomery City Lines, the city's African American residents prepared to reclaim their seats on the bus. On December 21, King, Abernathy, and Nixon boarded a local bus for the first time in 381 days.

King, who sat near the front of the bus, rode alongside a white Methodist minister and civil rights leader named Glenn Smiley. The pair made Montgomery history for becoming the city's first integrated bus riders. Yet King was not naive. He warned former boycotters that they would undoubtedly face intolerance and unkindness and advised

Martin Luther King Jr. (second row on left) rides a Montgomery city bus on December 21, 1956, at the end of the yearlong boycott.

them to respond peacefully. King likewise urged Montgomery's African American population to adopt the perspective that desegregation was not so much a triumph over whites as it was an opportunity for building better relations between both races.

"We cannot be satisfied with a court 'victory' over our white brothers," he explained. "We must respond to the [Supreme Court's] decision with an understanding of those who have oppressed us and with an appreciation of the new adjustments that the court order poses for them. We must be able to face up honestly to our own shortcomings. We must act in such a way as to make possible a coming together of white people and colored people on the basis of a real harmony of interests and understanding. We seek an integration based on mutual respect."

King's words resounded within Montgomery's African American community, but not everyone heeded his advice on the heels of the boycott. For example, the WCC encouraged white riders to stay off public transportation after it became integrated. In January 1957 a group of Montgomery businessmen even briefly proposed forming a private bus company that would exclusively service white passengers.

Following the integration of city buses, members of the KKK incited violence and terror throughout Montgomery. Reports of bombs thrown at black churches and the homes of well-known civil rights activists started circulating not long after the Supreme Court's ruling was enforced. Accounts of African American bus riders being harassed, beaten, and shot at prompted one local journalist to note that the city was "already paying a grievous toll" for desegregating public transportation.

The perpetrators of such violence were rarely charged with a crime, and if they were, they seldom faced conviction in southern courts, which continued to favor segregation. Black activists, on the other hand, generally had a different experience when they were brought before local or state judges. For instance, the Alabama Court of Appeals upheld Rosa Parks's conviction from December 1955, when she had been found guilty of violating bus segregation laws.

Despite the Supreme Court's decision, numerous Montgomery lawmakers and judges declined to disregard the Jim Crow laws. In fact, several members of the city's white

Rosa Parks and other riders of both races board a bus at the end of the boycott.

community continued to use whatever methods were available to them to maintain a racially segregated society. From their point of view, desegregation threatened an established social order that had existed in Montgomery for years.

Comments from white bus riders, such as "I would rather die and go to hell than sit behind a nigger" and "What are these niggers gonna do next," were not uncommon. This reaction, however, was not universal. Though fewer white passengers patronized the Montgomery City Lines in the months following the Supreme Court's ruling, those who did were often calm, quiet, and polite even though they were unaccustomed to the new seating arrangement.

But no matter what perspective Montgomery's white residents held, life would never be the same for them or for African Americans across the country in the wake of the boycott. While southern buses became increasingly integrated, the years ahead were filled with different yet equally intense struggles for civil rights activists. The civil rights movement that took root when Rosa Parks refused to give up her seat strengthened and advanced throughout the nation during the 1950s and 1960s. As it did—and decades after it concluded—U.S. citizens developed new viewpoints on the significance of the Montgomery Bus Boycott and its role in reshaping American society.

Six
A Lasting Legacy

From the perspective of many of the men and women who had participated in the bus boycott, integrating public transportation in Montgomery was a monumental milestone in the civil rights movement. At the same time, however, America—and especially the South—was far from desegregated. When deciding *Browder v. Gayle,* the Supreme Court had ruled against "separate but equal" statutes in regard to public transportation. Yet African Americans still faced routine discrimination in settings ranging from voting booths to swimming pools.

For Martin Luther King Jr., the Montgomery Bus Boycott was evidence that such situations could be overcome using peaceful but persuasive tactics. Having gained recognition during this battle in Alabama, he soon was considered one of the leaders of the national civil rights movement. In this role, King encouraged activists to continue fighting segregation by participating in nonviolent protests. In addition to boycotts, other popular methods of protest during the late 1950s and early 1960s were demonstrations, rallies, marches, and sit-ins.

Activists remained persistent in their struggle to desegregate America. Many worked tirelessly to ensure that public schools and universities were truly integrated. Some protestors overturned policies that supported segregated lunch counters by staging sit-ins in the dining areas of well-known department stores, including Woolworth's. Others organized campaigns to eliminate practices that restricted African Americans from being able to vote, own real estate in certain areas, or take advantage of equal employment opportunities.

These efforts prompted several positive changes in a society that had accepted segregation for nearly a century. Yet, from the perspective of many activists, it was slow and challenging work. Even if a local statute or department store policy was altered to ensure that blacks received fairer treatment, enforcing desegregation was no simple matter.

Some white southerners maintained the attitude that lawmakers' opinions on racial integration were insignificant. These citizens often made no attempt to hide their determination to preserve their way of life, which was—and always had been—defined by segregation. White officials, police, and community leaders in southern towns and cities frequently supported each other in promoting this point of view.

Because of resistance to desegregation, Supreme Court rulings were slow to improve the lives of African Americans. Many southern schools, businesses, and public facilities and services continued to oppose integration. As hundreds of activists discovered in 1961, the same philosophy also endured when it came to interstate transportation companies.

In May of that year, both black and white supporters of the civil rights movement started boarding buses in Washington, DC, that were headed to various southern cities. The purpose of these journeys, which were commonly called Freedom Rides, was to test the effectiveness of the 1960

Freedom Riders arrive in Montgomery under the protection of police and the National Guard in May 1961.

Supreme Court decision known as *Boynton v. Virginia*. The issue at stake was whether laws segregating interstate bus and railway stations were constitutional. Though *Boynton v. Virginia* ordered the desegregation of such areas, activists doubted how strictly their ruling was being enforced throughout the South.

The Freedom Riders quickly saw firsthand that segregation was still commonplace at numerous southern bus and railway stations. In addition, they received hostile treatment from whites who continued to promote a segregated society.

Activists were frequently attacked with clubs, chains, and even bombs. Several Freedom Riders were also arrested on charges that included trespassing, unlawfully assembling, and violating various Jim Crow statutes.

From the civil rights activists' perspective, however, their suffering was not in vain. As President John F. Kennedy and his brother U.S. Attorney General Robert Kennedy learned of the Freedom Riders' struggles, they began pushing for tougher federal enforcement of desegregation laws. Consequently, the Interstate Commerce Commission (ICC), a federal agency that regulates the transportation of goods and people between U.S. states, cracked down on segregation in bus terminals and railway stations.

In September 1961, the ICC outlawed this type of discrimination with a set of rules that were more specific and more strictly enforced than those the Supreme Court included in its *Boynton v. Virginia* decision. The Freedom Riders maintained that the risks they took—just like those taken by boycotters in Montgomery years before—were necessary. They believed that if they backed down, the civil rights movement would never move forward, and segregation would never end on buses, at lunch counters, or in thousands of other settings across America.

As Diane Nash, a Freedom Rider and civil rights activist, explained, "I strongly felt that the future of the [civil rights] movement was going to be cut short if the Freedom Rides had been stopped as a result of violence." She further explained that the public impression would have been "that whenever a movement starts, all that has to be done is . . . attack it with massive violence, and the blacks [will] stop." Over time, though, it became clear that activists were not willing to stop, and neither were a growing number of federal officials.

Presidential Perspectives

During the 1960s national debate surrounding segregation intensified. A few civil rights activists were even murdered by people who were angered by their interference in communities far from their homes. One of the most infamous examples of this was King's assassination in Memphis, Tennessee, in April 1968.

In the years before King's death, the civil rights leader and his fellow activists witnessed the federal government's increasingly noticeable role in supporting and enforcing desegregation laws. Prior to the 1960s the promotion of racial equality seldom concerned U.S. presidents. Few presidents up to that point had lived during eras that featured political movements in which an overwhelming number of citizens united to protest racial discrimination. Before Kennedy, several American leaders had been guided by the opinion that the time was coming to modify segregation laws, but they were hesitant to move too fast or act too drastically.

"I believe that we should not stagnate, but again I plead for understanding, for really sympathetic consideration of the problem that is far larger, both in emotional and even its physical aspects, than most of us realize," stated Dwight Eisenhower in 1956. Eisenhower, who served as president from 1953 to 1961, was explaining his views on desegregating public transportation in response to the Montgomery Bus Boycott.

"There are emotions, very deep emotions, connected with this problem," he continued. "As far as I am concerned,

Kennedy and Civil Rights

In June 1963 President Kennedy addressed the nation on the need for civil rights legislation that would end segregation and the national unrest that was resulting from it. "The fires of frustration and discord are burning in every city, North and South, where legal remedies are not at hand," he declared. "Redress is sought in the streets, in demonstrations, parades, and protests which create tensions and threaten violence and threaten lives."

About a week later, Kennedy spoke to members of Congress on this same issue. "No one has been barred on account of his race from fighting or dying for America," he observed. "There are no 'white' or 'coloreds' signs on the foxholes or graveyards of battle." The Civil Rights Act was not passed until after his death, but Kennedy was one of the first presidents to speak out against segregation.

SEAL OF THE PRESIDENT OF THE UNITED STATES

I am for moderation, but I am for progress; that is exactly what I am for in this thing." Kennedy, who was elected after Eisenhower, took a somewhat more decisive stand against segregation. In the wake of the Montgomery Bus Boycott, the civil rights movement grew stronger, and the public outcry for change became more pronounced. At the same time, so did unrest and violence.

The Supreme Court handed down an increasing number of decisions that outlawed segregation during these years. President Kennedy started deploying federal troops to protect activists such as the Freedom Riders and to ensure that African Americans everywhere were allowed to take advantage of newly integrated public programming. Kennedy also favored the legislation that became the Civil Rights Act of 1964.

Though Kennedy was assassinated in late 1963 before this bill received congressional approval, his perspective on the need to desegregate America was shared by his successor, Lyndon B. Johnson. Thanks largely to Johnson's encouragement, Congress finally voted in favor of federal legislation that fundamentally declared segregation to be illegal. The Civil Rights Act, signed into law in July 1964, outlawed discrimination in public places. In addition, it granted the federal government the authority to enforce the desegregation of schools and other public facilities. Finally, the Civil Rights Act prohibited employers from displaying discriminatory behavior within the workplace and restricted the use of literacy tests as a requirement for voter registration.

In addition to safeguarding the rights of African Americans, this act also forbade discrimination based on a person's gender, religion, or ethnic background. Slightly less than

President Lyndon B. Johnson signs the Civil Rights Act on July 2, 1964.

nine years after the Montgomery Bus Boycott, the defining principles of that protest had become the foundation of a new federal law. The Civil Rights Act essentially ordered that all citizens be guaranteed the freedoms and privileges outlined in the U.S. Constitution.

As Johnson proclaimed during a radio and television broadcast to the nation in July 1964:

> This Civil Rights Act is a challenge to all of us to go to work in our communities and our States, in our homes and in our hearts, to eliminate the last vestiges of injustice in our beloved country. So tonight I urge every public official, every religious leader, every business and professional man, every workingman, every housewife—I urge every American—to join in this effort to bring justice and hope to all our people—and to bring peace to our land. . . . Let us close the springs of racial poison. Let us pray for wise and understanding hearts. Let us lay aside irrelevant differences and make our Nation whole.

Many Americans believe these goals have yet to be fully reached. Some argue that even after the civil rights movement wound down during the late 1960s, blacks continued to face discrimination and still do. Opinions on this issue remain divided, as do perspectives on how the Montgomery Bus Boycott is remembered decades after it triggered U.S. citizens to reevaluate their views on segregation.

Keeping the Dream Alive

In December 2005 politicians, activists, journalists, and average Americans commemorated the fiftieth anniversary of the boycott. Though a handful of the protest's participants were still alive to share their recollections and experiences, many others were not, including Rosa Parks, who had died the previous October.

A teenager places roses on a bust of Rosa Parks at the Rosa Parks Museum in Montgomery.

Whether racial discrimination has been completely eliminated may be debatable, but no one today is arrested for sitting in the wrong seat on the bus, nor have many been threatened for anything to do with public transportation. According to Ray White, vice chancellor of Montgomery's Troy University, the time that has elapsed since the bus boycott occurred has led America's youth to lose touch with the magnitude and realities of this event. White arrived at such a conclusion after several years of regularly interacting with members of the public who visit the Rosa Parks Library and Museum, which is located on Troy's campus.

"Based on over 350,000 visitors touring the Rosa Parks Museum, my experience in listening to many of the young people is that most . . . don't know the history of the Montgomery Bus Boycott, and they know very little in-depth history about civil rights in general," he noted during a 2010 interview. "They know the names of the major figures such as Dr. Martin Luther King Jr., Rosa Parks, and maybe a few know Ralph Abernathy or E. D. Nixon. Very few really know much about what they did to fight racial injustices."

He further explained that it is this lack of knowledge that makes it difficult for modern generations to grasp what activists endured in their battle to end segregation on southern buses. "If there is one thing I've learned in the ten years the Rosa Parks Museum has been open," said White, "it is that most of our society does not really know the history of the civil rights movement. If they don't know it, they can't fully appreciate the sacrifices made by the civil rights leaders." Johnnie Rebecca Daniels Carr, who helped organize the boycott and headed the MIA from 1967 until her death in 2008, concurred with this perspective. Carr dedicated most of her life following the protest to publicly speaking about her experiences in Montgomery and about activists' struggles to overcome segregation.

"I spend much of my time educating people about what happened back in the 1950s," Carr said in 2004. "Unless we tell them, the young people won't know about the struggles and the hardships we went through to get what we have today. We've come a long, long way, but we've also got a lot to do to keep the dream alive." From White's point of view, the dream can and should be kept alive through collecting and publishing the testimonials of boycott participants. He also believes that schools, museums, and community organizations should offer additional programming to provide students with a more comprehensive view of the civil rights movement.

"We can be a better society when our next generation knows and appreciates what those who preceded them experienced and how they sacrificed," White remarked. "If young people know and understand the struggles and sacrifices of the civil rights movement, they can be stronger and more determined to do their part in helping their generation and future generations treat each other with dignity and respect." This goal will undoubtedly ensure that the Montgomery Bus Boycott is never forgotten. If Americans continue to protect the civil rights legacy shaped by the countless individuals who banded together and stood up to segregation starting in December 1955, it will remain an enduring and influential lesson for centuries to come.

Timeline

1865–1870 Congress passes the Thirteenth, Fourteenth, and Fifteenth amendments—commonly referred to as the Reconstruction, or Civil War, Amendments—primarily to guarantee the full rights of citizenship to African Americans.

1876 Southern cities begin enacting a series of segregationist statutes known as Jim Crow laws.

1896 U.S. Supreme Court justices hand down a ruling in *Plessy v. Ferguson* that promotes a "separate but equal" doctrine in regard to racial segregation.

May 1954 The Supreme Court decision in *Brown v. Board of Education* declares that the "separate but equal" doctrine is unconstitutional.

December 1, 1955 Rosa Parks is arrested for violating local segregation laws when she refuses to give up her seat to accommodate a white passenger while riding the Montgomery City Lines in Montgomery, Alabama.

December 5, 1955 Activists begin a 381-day boycott of the Montgomery City Lines to protest Parks's arrest and the segregated seating policies on public transportation; leaders within the black community form the Montgomery Improvement Association (MIA) this same day.

February 1, 1956 Fred Gray and Charles Langford file a lawsuit (*Browder v. Gayle*) in Montgomery's federal district court; referring to the Fourteenth Amendment, they ask the court to declare local bus segregation laws unconstitutional.

June 19, 1956 The federal district court issues its official opinion in *Browder v. Gayle,* with two out of three judges declaring that Montgomery's bus segregation laws are unconstitutional.

November 13, 1956 Supreme Court justices uphold the ruling originally handed down by federal district court judges the previous June in *Browder v. Gayle.*

December 20, 1956 The MIA declares the boycott to be at an end when an official notice containing the Supreme Court's orders to integrate local buses arrives in Montgomery.

December 21, 1956 Members of the city's black community, including Martin Luther King Jr., Ralph Abernathy, and E. D. Nixon, board public transportation for the first time in 381 days.

May 1961 Civil rights activists known as Freedom Riders begin a series of bus trips throughout the South. Their goal is to test the effectiveness of the 1960 Supreme Court ruling in *Boynton v. Virginia,* which outlawed segregation in interstate bus and railway stations. The violence these activists encounter results in the federal government's becoming more involved in promoting and upholding desegregation laws.

July 1964 In what is considered one of the most significant victories of the civil rights movement, President Lyndon B. Johnson signs the Civil Rights Act into law. This legislation illegalizes discrimination in public settings and grants the federal government added authority to enforce the desegregation of schools and other public facilities. In addition, it prohibits employers from displaying discriminatory behavior within the workplace.

Notes

Chapter 1

p. 11, "refusing to obey [the] orders . . .": wording of police report describing charges filed against Rosa Parks on December 1, 1955, "Teaching with Documents: An Act of Courage, the Arrest Records of Rosa Parks," U.S. National Archives, date of last update not available, www.archives.gov/education/lessons/rosa-parks/ (accessed June 26, 2010).

p. 11, "I had no idea . . .": Rosa Parks, quoted in Mark Feeney, "Rosa Parks, Civil Rights Icon, Dead at 92," *Boston Globe*, October 25, 2005, www.boston.com/news/nation/articles/2005/10/25/rosa_parks_civil_rights_icon_dead_at_92/ (accessed June 26, 2010).

p. 12, "When I got on the . . .": Rosa Parks, quoted in Donnie Williams with Wayne Greenhaw, *The Thunder of Angels* (Chicago: Lawrence Hill Books, 2006), pp. 47–48.

p. 21, "We consider the underlying . . .": Henry Billings Brown, "African Americans after Slavery," University of Houston: Digital History, June 26, 2010, www.digitalhistory.uh.edu/historyonline/us22.cfm (accessed June 26, 2010).

p. 21, "to promote equality of rights . . .": wording of pledge of the National Association for the Advancement of Colored People (NAACP), "NAACP: A Century in the Fight for Freedom," Library of Congress, date last updated not available, www.myloc.gov/Exhibitions/naacp/Pages/Themes.aspx (accessed June 26, 2010).

p. 23, "We conclude that, in the . . . :" Earl Warren, "Supreme Court of the United States, *Brown v. Board of Education*, 347 U.S. 483 (1954) (USSC+)," National Center for Public

Policy Research, May 17, 1954, www.nationalcenter.org/brown.html (accessed June 26, 2010).

Chapter 2

p. 29, "This is for Monday, December 5 . . .": wording of handbill produced to publicize the start of the Montgomery Bus Boycott, quoted in Ken Hare, "Overview," *The Montgomery Advertiser: The Story of the Montgomery Bus Boycott,* June 7, 2005, www.montgomeryboycott.com/article_overview.htm (accessed June 26, 2010).

p. 35, "to improve the general status . . .": Martin Luther King Jr., quoted in Williams, *The Thunder of Angels,* p. 197.

p. 37, "When he heard me . . .": E. D. Nixon, quoted in Williams, *The Thunder of Angels,* p. 60.

p. 39, "There comes a time when . . .": Martin Luther King Jr., "Rosa Parks: Part B," Smithsonian Center for Education and Museum Studies, date last updated not available, www.smithsoniansource.org/display/lesson/viewdetails.aspx?LessonPlanId=1003&LessonId=1004 (accessed June 26, 2010).

Chapter 3

p. 41, "the white folks will kill . . .": Raymond Parks, quoted in Rosalind Rosenberg, *Divided Lives: American Women in the Twentieth Century* (New York: Hill and Wang, 1992), p. 174.

p. 42, "courteous treatment on the buses . . .": wording of demands that leaders of the Montgomery Improvement Association (MIA) presented to Montgomery officials and representatives of the Montgomery City Lines, "The Montgomery

Bus Boycott," Alabama Department of Archives and History, date last updated not available, www.alabamamoments.state.al.us/sec55det.html (accessed June 26, 2010).

p. 42, "Surely the world will see . . .": Ralph Abernathy, quoted in Williams, *The Thunder of Angels*, p. 111.

p. 43, "reforms of existing rules . . .": Martin Luther King Jr., quoted in Williams, *The Thunder of Angels*, p. 110.

p. 45, "Although we raised a lot . . .": E. D. Nixon, quoted in Williams, *The Thunder of Angels*, p. 114.

p. 47, "hoodwinked": Martin Luther King Jr., quoted in Williams, *The Thunder of Angels*, p. 117.

p. 48, "Those people were so . . .": Montgomery journalist covering the bombing of Martin Luther King Jr.'s home in early 1956, quoted in Williams, *The Thunder of Angels*, p. 134.

p. 49, "All persons born or naturalized . . .": wording of the Fourteenth Amendment, "14th Amendment," Cornell University Law School: Legal Information Institute, date last updated not available, www.topics.law.cornell.edu/constitution/amendmentxiv (accessed June 26, 2010).

p. 52, "wanted the court to have . . .": Fred Gray, "*Browder v. Gayle*, 352 U.S. 903 (1956)," Stanford University's Martin Luther King, Jr., Research and Education Institute, date last updated not available, http://mlk-kpp01.stanford.edu/index.php/encyclopedia/encyclopedia/enc_browder_v_gayle/ (accessed June 26, 2010).

p. 52, "Frankly, I am for . . .": Martin Luther King Jr., quoted in Williams, *The Thunder of Angels*, p. 112.

Chapter 4

p. 55, "who have split asunder . . .": William Gayle, quoted in Williams, *The Thunder of Angels*, p. 118.

p. 56, "the social fabric of our . . .": William Gayle, quoted in Williams, *The Thunder of Angels*, p. 118.

p. 56, "This bunch of niggers . . .": Clyde Sellers, quoted in Williams, *The Thunder of Angels*, p. 111.

p. 57, "Southern way of life . . .": members of the White Citizens' Council (WCC) in favor of preserving segregation laws, "White Citizens' Councils Aimed to Maintain 'Southern Way of Life,'" *Jackson Sun*, date last updated not available, http://.orig.jacksonsun.com/civilrights/sec2_citizencouncil.shtml (accessed June 26, 2010).

p. 58, "I think every right-thinking . . .": William Gayle, "White Citizens' Councils," Stanford University's Martin Luther King, Jr., Research and Education Institute, date last updated not available, www.mlk-kpp01.stanford.edu/index.php/encyclopedia/encyclopedia/enc_white_citizens_councils_wcc/ (accessed June 27, 2010).

p. 58, "Like Mayor Gayle said . . .": Terry Leon Hall, quoted in Williams, The Thunder of Angels, pp. 127–128.

p. 59, "The niggers are getting . . .": Sam Engelhardt, quoted in Williams, *The Thunder of Angels*, p. 126.

p. 62, "illegally running a taxi . . .": wording of charges police attempted to level against Robert Graetz for participating in the MIA-sponsored car pool, quoted in Williams, *The Thunder of Angels*, p. 144.

p. 62, "People either loved us or . . .": Robert Graetz, quoted in Jannell McGrew, "Rev. Robert Graetz," *The Montgomery Advertiser: The Story of the Montgomery Bus Boycott*, June 7, 2005, www.montgomeryboycott.com/article_overview.htm (accessed June 29, 2010).

p. 63, "The bus boycott, you have . . .": Robert Graetz, quoted in McGrew, "Rev. Robert Graetz," www.montgomeryboycott.com/article_overview.htm (accessed June 29, 2010).

p. 64, "The Negroes are laughing at . . .": William Gayle, quoted in Williams, *The Thunder of Angels*, p. 119.

p. 64, "The Negroes have made . . .": William Gayle, quoted in Williams, *The Thunder of Angels*, p. 119.

p. 64, "protect them from [the] harassment . . .": white housewives in Montgomery who drove their African American domestic help to and from work during the boycott, quoted in Stephen E. Frantzich, *Citizen Democracy: Political Activists in a Cynical Age* (Lanham, MD: Rowman and Littlefield, 2005), p. 42.

Chapter 5

p. 67, "As far as I'm concerned . . .": Frank Johnson Jr., quoted in Williams, *The Thunder of Angels*, p. 218.

p. 67, "I don't reach it that . . .": Seybourn Lynne, quoted in Williams, *The Thunder of Angels*, p. 218.

p. 68, "We hold that the . . .": wording of official written opinion of federal district court judges in Montgomery who presided over *Browder v. Gayle*, quoted in Williams, *The Thunder of Angels*, p. 220.

p. 69, 'They may do their best . . .": Frank Johnson Jr.,

quoted in Williams, *The Thunder of Angels*, p. 258.

p. 69, "forfeited the right to be . . .": Montgomery journalist speaking of Richard Rives, quoted in Williams, *The Thunder of Angels*, p. 259.

p. 70, "the streets . . . for the construction . . .": attorneys representing Montgomery who objected to the legality of the MIA-sponsored car pool, quoted in Williams, *The Thunder of Angels*, p. 237.

p. 70, "Through their unity, their carpools . . .": J. E. Pierce, quoted in Williams, *The Thunder of Angels*, p. 233.

p. 72, "a glorious daybreak to end . . .": Martin Luther King Jr., quoted in Williams, *The Thunder of Angels*, p. 239.

p. 72, "insists on disrupting our . . .": Sam Engelhardt, quoted in Williams, *The Thunder of Angels*, p. 244.

p. 73, "We cannot be satisfied . . .": Martin Luther King Jr., quoted in Williams, *The Thunder of Angels*, pp. 253–254.

p. 74, "already paying a grievous . . .": Montgomery journalist commenting on violence resulting from the integration of city buses, quoted in Williams, *The Thunder of Angels*, p. 262.

p. 75, "I would rather die . . .": wording of commonly cited response from white passengers to the integration of Montgomery buses, quoted in Clayborne Carson, ed., *The Autobiography of Martin Luther King, Jr.* (New York: Warner Books, 2001), p. 98.

p. 75, "What are these niggers . . .": quoted in Carson, *The Autobiography of Martin Luther King, Jr.*, p. 98.

Chapter 6

p. 80, "I strongly felt that . . .": Diane Nash, quoted in Wesley C. Hogan, *Many Minds, One Heart: SNCC's Dream for a New America* (Chapel Hill: University of North Carolina Press, 2007), 47.

p. 81, "that whenever a movement . . .": quoted in Hogan, *Many Minds, One Heart: SNCC's Dream for a New America*, p. 47.

p. 81, "I believe that we . . .": Dwight D. Eisenhower, quoted in Williams, *The Thunder of Angels*, p. 200.

p. 82, "The fires of frustration . . .": John F. Kennedy, quoted in Philip A. Klinkner with Rogers M. Smith, *The Unsteady March: The Rise and Decline of Racial Equality in America* (Chicago: University of Chicago Press, 1999), p. 268.

p. 82, "No one has been . . .": John F. Kennedy, quoted in Klinkner, *The Unsteady March: The Rise and Decline of Racial Equality in America*, p. 269.

p. 84, "There are emotions . . .": Dwight D. Eisenhower, quoted in Williams, *The Thunder of Angels*, pp. 201–202.

p. 86, "This Civil Rights Act is . . .": Lyndon B. Johnson, "President Lyndon B. Johnson's Radio and Television Remarks upon Signing the Civil Rights Bill, July 2, 1964," The Lyndon Baines Johnson Library and Museum, June 6, 2007, www.lbjlib.utexas.edu/johnson/archives.hom/speeches.hom/640702.asp (accessed June 27, 2010).

p. 88, "Based on over 350,000 . . .": Ray White, quoted in interview conducted by author on June 22, 2010.

p. 88, "If there is one thing . . .": Ray White, quoted in interview conducted by author on June 22, 2010.

p. 89, "I spend much of my . . .": Johnnie Rebecca Daniels Carr, quoted in Williams, *The Thunder of Angels*, p. 270.
p. 89, "We can be a better . . .": Ray White, quoted in interview conducted by author on June 22, 2010.

Further Information

Books

Aretha, David. *Montgomery Bus Boycott*. Greensboro, NC: Morgan Reynolds, 2009.

Ashby, Ruth. *Rosa Parks: Freedom Rider*. New York: Sterling, 2008.

Colbert, David. *Ten Days: Martin Luther King Jr.* New York: Simon and Schuster, 2009.

Gold, Susan Dudley. *Civil Rights Act of 1964*. New York: Marshall Cavendish Benchmark, 2011.

Hardy, Sheila, and P. Stephen Hardy. *Extraordinary People of the Civil Rights Movement*. New York: Children's Press, 2007.

DVD

Boycott. HBO Films, 2001.

Websites

***The Montgomery Advertiser*—The Story of the Montgomery Bus Boycott**

www.montgomeryboycott.com

A website with a timeline, biographical accounts, and archived newspaper articles related to the boycott.

The Rosa and Raymond Parks Institute for Self-Development

www.rosaparks.org/

An online resource containing information about the famous civil rights activist and her efforts to end segregation.

Time Magazine—_Time_ Collection: Civil Rights

www.time.com/time/archive/collections/0,21428,c_civil_rights,00.shtml

A website featuring an extensive collection of archived magazine articles discussing the civil rights movement.

Bibliography

Books

Carson, Clayborne, ed. *The Autobiography of Martin Luther King, Jr.* New York: Warner Books, 2001.

Frantzich, Stephen E. *Citizen Democracy: Political Activists in a Cynical Age*. Lanham, MD: Rowman and Littlefield, 2005.

Hogan, Wesley C. *Many Minds, One Heart: SNCC's Dream for a New America*. Chapel Hill: University of North Carolina Press, 2007.

Klinkner, Philip A., with Rogers M. Smith. *The Unsteady March: The Rise and Decline of Racial Equality in America*. Chicago: University of Chicago Press, 1999.

Rosenberg, Rosalind. *Divided Lives: American Women in the Twentieth Century*. New York: Hill and Wang, 1992.

Williams, Donnie, with Wayne Greenhaw. *The Thunder of Angels*. Chicago: Lawrence Hill Books, 2006.

Interview

Interview conducted with Ray White by author on June 22, 2010.

Online Articles

"African Americans after Slavery," University of Houston:

Digital History, June 26, 2010. www.digitalhistory.uh.edu/historyonline/us22.cfm (accessed June 26, 2010).

"*Browder v. Gayle*, 352 U.S. 903 (1956)," Martin Luther King, Jr., Research and Education Institute, date last updated not available. http://mlk-kpp01.stanford.edu/index.php/encyclopedia/encyclopedia/enc_browder_v_gayle/ (accessed June 26, 2010).

Feeney, Mark. "Rosa Parks, Civil Rights Icon, Dead at 92," *Boston Globe*, October 25, 2005. www.boston.com/news/nation/articles/2005/10/25/rosa_parks_civil_rights_icon_dead_at_92/ (accessed June 26, 2010).

"14th Amendment," Cornell University Law School: Legal Information Institute, date last updated not available. http://topics.law.cornell.edu/constitution/amendmentxiv (accessed June 26, 2010).

Hare, Ken. "Overview," *The Montgomery Advertiser: The Story of the Montgomery Bus Boycott*, June 7, 2005. www.montgomeryboycott.com/article_overview.htm (accessed June 26, 2010).

McGrew, Jannell. "Rev. Robert Graetz," *The Montgomery Advertiser: The Story of the Montgomery Bus Boycott*, June 7, 2005. www.montgomeryboycott.com/profile_graetz.htm (accessed June 29, 2010).

"The Montgomery Bus Boycott," Alabama Department of Archives and History, date last updated not available. www.alabamamoments.state.al.us/sec55det.html (accessed June 26, 2010).

"NAACP: A Century in the Fight for Freedom," Library of Congress, date last updated not available. www.myloc.gov/Exhibitions/naacp/Pages/Themes.aspx (accessed June 26, 2010).

"President Lyndon B. Johnson's Radio and Television Remarks upon Signing the Civil Rights Bill, July 2, 1964," Lyndon Baines Johnson Library and Museum, June 6, 2007. www.lbjlib.utexas.edu/johnson/archives.hom/speeches.hom/640702.asp (accessed June 27, 2010).

"Rosa Parks: Part B," Smithsonian Center for Education and Museum Studies, date last updated not available. www.smithsoniansource.org/display/lesson/viewdetails.aspx?LessonPlanId=1003&LessonId=1004 (accessed June 26, 2010).

"Supreme Court of the United States, *Brown v. Board of Education*, 347 U.S. 483 (1954) (USSC+)," National Center for Public Policy Research, May 17, 1954. www.nationalcenter.org/brown.html (accessed June 26, 2010).

"Teaching with Documents: An Act of Courage, the Arrest Records of Rosa Parks," National Archives, date last updated not available. www.archives.gov/education/lessons/rosa-parks/ (accessed June 26, 2010).

"White Citizens' Councils Aimed to Maintain 'Southern Way of Life,'" *Jackson Sun*, date last updated not available. http://orig.jacksonsun.com/civilrights/sec2_citizencouncil.shtml (accessed June 26, 2010).

Index

Page numbers in **boldface** are illustrations.

About the Author

Katie Marsico is the author of more than sixty reference books for children and young adults. Prior to becoming a full-time writer, she worked as a managing editor in publishing. She resides near Chicago, Illinois, with her husband, daughter, and two sons.